ANIMALS AND THEIR HOMES

SOME THREATS AND WAYS TO HELP

A Loving Earth Book

Loving Earth Project

lovingearth-project.uk

G000295177

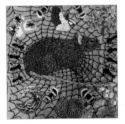  

ANIMALS AND THEIR HOMES
SOME THREATS AND WAYS TO HELP

We humans do amazing things for the sake of love. Think of what we do to prevent harm to our children, or the risks people take in wartime or to help others in emergency situations.

However, we are finding it very difficult to address the threats posed by climate and environmental changes. We know that the longer we delay action, the harder and faster catastrophes will hit. But even as we experience more heatwaves, droughts, floods, and storms, many of us fail to take serious action to adapt to these changes or reduce the harm we are causing. Truthful political leadership is lacking, and short-term or financial interests continue to dominate, at the expense of the long-term health of humans and animals worldwide, with poorer communities and wildlife suffering most of all.

None of us is going to solve the crisis alone, but we can all be part of the solution. The Loving Earth Project is helping people to engage with some of these issues, and to respond, inspired by love. Hundreds of people have found that thinking about something we love (a place, a person, a creature) and how environmental change

will affect it in the next two or three decades, helps us to discern how our own activities contribute to the threat and what we can do to adapt and help limit the damage.

Making a small textile artwork provides a fruitful way to explore and express these responses; it can lead to new conversations and learning. We have invited people to make textile squares in a standard size of 30×30cm, using any styles and techniques they like. Participants range from skilled textile artists to young children, and many have learned new textile skills as well as facts about environmental issues, the impact of their actions, and possible changes they can make. Most people have used scraps or re-used materials, and each maker has also written a short text to accompany their panel.

Creating a textile panel will not change the world, but it may change us. It may give us hope, energy, and motivation to act. It helps if we take time to attend to what we love, learn more about environmental threats, and take responsibility for our actions, one step at a time. The artworks we have created can remind us why this matters, strengthen our resolve, and inspire others.

This book presents a selection of panels that illustrate some of the creatures that panel-makers love, and what is happening to the places where they live. In writing this book, we have also drawn heavily on what other panel-makers have written as well as on external sources. The original texts for each panel can be seen in the online gallery at lovingearth-project.uk; they include personal stories, spiritual insights, and a range of scientific and practical information. The original titles of each panel are listed on page 74.

From oceans to hedgerows, icecaps to deserts, these habitats and the creatures that live on planet Earth are under threat. Like us, this beautiful world is both strong and fragile. It is only by learning more about what is happening, and by choosing to adapt in good time, that we will be able to help prevent worse damage to this wondrous world and its diverse inhabitants.

You can find out more about the Loving Earth Project on our website at **lovingearth-project.uk**. If you would like to join, the website has many online resources to help individuals and groups.

We hope that you enjoy the book, and that it inspires you and others to act.

Matt Rosen, Linda Murgatroyd, Rici Marshall Cross
Quaker Arts Network, September 2022

LIFE ON EARTH

Humans have so far catalogued about 1.6 million species of life on Earth; there may be another 7 or 8 million species still to be discovered. This biodiversity is essential for human survival and for making life worth living. Yet it is under intense pressure. Humanity has already caused the loss of 83% of all wild mammals and half of plant species. Global warming, brought about largely by industrial activities and burning fossil fuels, affects the entire world and all the creatures that call it home.

Our individual actions can make a difference, but we also need to work together with communities and organisations around the world to use land and water wisely and protect the vulnerable.

The maker of this panel undertook to reduce her carbon footprint, to work with others on combatting local pesticide and herbicide use, and to explore further how privilege is linked to the freedom to choose how to live.

"Let us all commit ourselves to doing our part to help make a positive difference to the environment of our only common home, this beautiful Earth."
—Tenzin Gyatso, the Dalai Lama, 2021

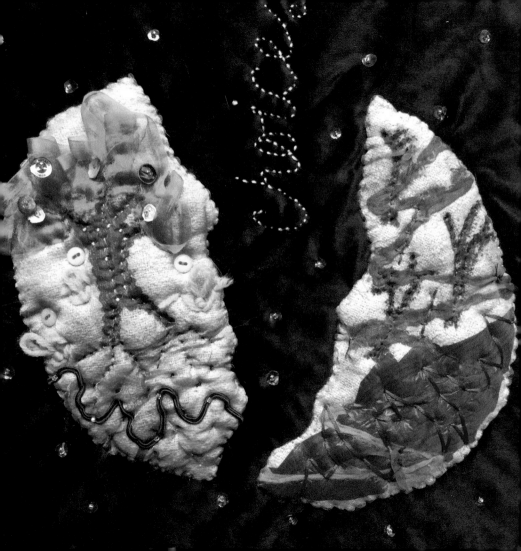

WATER

Water covers two-thirds of the Earth's surface; over 97% of this is salt water in seas and oceans. Water is home to many of the oldest known species on our planet, from some of the largest to many of the smallest. Oysters, for example, appeared between 150 and 200 million years ago, whereas humans have been around for only 5 to 7 million years.

Climate change is causing ocean temperatures to rise, and mass coral bleaching events are becoming more frequent. Nearly half the corals in the Great Barrier Reef died in 2016 and 2017. Carbon dioxide absorbed into the oceans from the atmosphere is causing acidification. This alters seawater chemistry, reducing calcification in reef-building organisms, shellfish, and other creatures.

Ocean acidification is among the greatest threats, not only to life in our oceans, but also to life on land and in the air.

So we all need to cut our net carbon emissions. The website **carbonindependent.org** can help us with this. Some wider issues are discussed on p68-71.

SEA TURTLES & PLASTICS

More than 4,000 turtles die each year as a direct result of ocean pollution. Their numbers are falling sharply. Seabirds, seals, dolphins, whales, and other sea creatures are also being harmed by this.

Plastic is a big part of the problem: eight million tonnes of plastic are leaking into our oceans each year. 40% of this comes from shipping or fishing. Other plastics come downstream from rivers, sewers, and industrial waste. Over 26,000 tonnes of plastic waste is estimated to have been added to the ocean in the first two years of the COVID-19 pandemic alone.

Plastic debris and synthetic fabrics eventually break down into tiny fragments, and some microplastics are also needlessly used in cosmetics and cleaning products. Seen from the bottom of the ocean, things don't look great.

WHALES

This panel highlights the issue of discarded single-use plastics and fishing tackle polluting the oceans. It was inspired by a video showing two divers trying to cut a rope and net off a whale. It took a long time to cut through the rope, but the whale stayed still. When it was finally free, it swam away from the divers; then it turned back, nudging the divers gently as if saying thank you.

Disoriented whales are regularly beached or lost, including upstream in rivers. Some collide with ships. Noise from ships, submarine sonar, and underwater blasting disrupt whales' ability to communicate and navigate. Changes in ocean chemistry and temperature from climate change and pollution also threaten the well-being of these magnificent, intelligent sea mammals.

We are only just starting to understand the important role whales play in maintaining healthy seas. Greenpeace, the United Nations, and others have campaigned to end whale-hunting, reduce pollution, and protect ocean environments, including by creating ocean sanctuaries. But some countries have so far been unwilling to sign up to this, and policing the oceans is a major challenge.

OVERFISHING: FISHING OVER

We have disrespected the ocean and the creatures that live in it. About 40% of marine life caught worldwide is caught as bycatch and thrown back into the ocean dead.

How 'sustainable' can it be to fish for cod in the North Atlantic, take it to China for processing, and sell it plastic-wrapped and frozen worldwide? Farmed fish are often harmed by parasites and disease, and fish farms are ruining coastal ecologies in many parts of the world.

The 2021 film *Seaspiracy* shows that the independence of the Marine Stewardship Council is questionable. Stronger international controls are needed to enforce sustainable fishing practices. Governments need to lead, and we can influence this as voters, but as consumers we can also put pressure on the companies involved. We can all learn how fish comes to our plate and think carefully about how much fish – if any – it is right for us to eat.

"We do not own the world, and its riches are not ours to dispose of at will."
—Quaker "Advices and Queries", 1994, No. 42

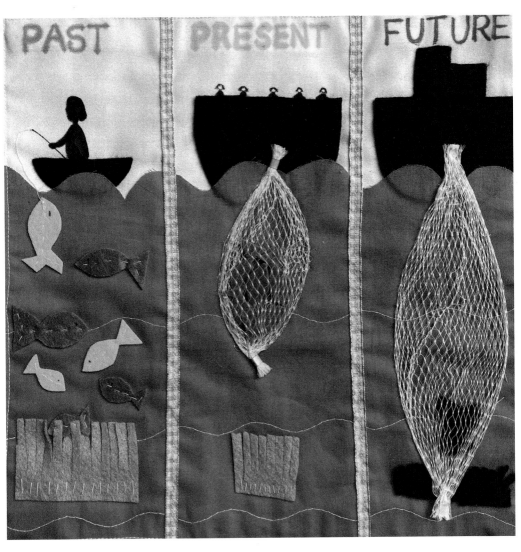

MORE THAN A CULINARY DELIGHT

Cuttlebones litter the shoreline where I live. When I tried to find out more about them, my heart began to sink. Cuttlefish and squid are exceptionally intelligent. But instead of considering them as an integral part of the natural world, to be respected, we catch them for food or their ink or keep them as pets. Cuttlefish landings have increased enormously over the last 50 years, even though they are on the Marine Conservation Society's red "endangered" list.

Many other populations of sea life are also on the verge of collapse. Only 1% of all international waters are protected in any way. Scientists say that we need to protect at least 30% of our oceans by 2030 to halt their decline. That means we need to act fast.

"Exercise goodness towards every living creature."

—John Woolman, 1774

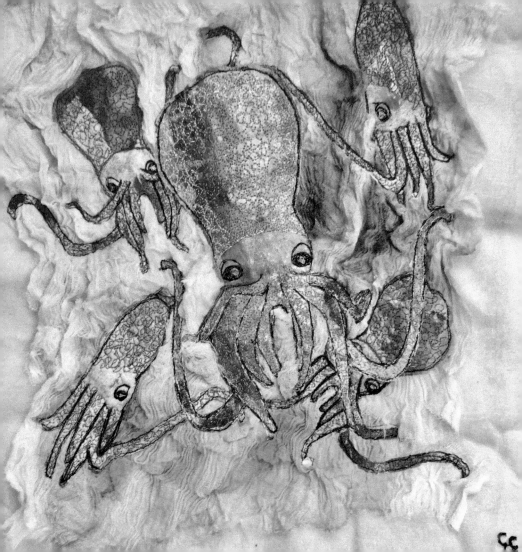

SEAGRASS

Underwater 'meadows' of seagrass provide food and shelter for a wide range of marine species. Lush, beautiful, and biodiverse, they remind me of the abundant life and clear waters of the coastline where I grew up.

Seagrass meadows absorb and store carbon more efficiently than rainforests, playing a key role in addressing climate change. They may also help limit coastal erosion by reducing wave energy. When seagrass meadows become damaged, carbon is released, adding to greenhouse gas emissions.

The UK has lost about 90% of its seagrass meadows due to disease and human impacts: pollution, dredging, fish-farming, and industrial fishing practices which damage the seafloor.

Now that we know how precious this habitat is, we must protect, restore, and replant these underwater meadows. For example, in Scotland, a promising new project (Restoration Forth, managed by the World Wildlife Fund) aims to restore some of the lost areas of seagrass. We can support such efforts financially or perhaps by volunteering as the maker of this panel intends.

ICECAPS & GLACIERS

If we lose the polar icecaps, polar bears, penguins, and other creatures will lose their homes. This is already happening faster than predicted.

Arctic sea ice is being lost at a rate of nearly 13% per decade, and the oldest and thickest sections of sea ice have declined by nearly 95% in the last 30 years. Almost 700 billion tonnes of ice melt each year because of global warming. That means that roughly ten Olympic swimming pools of melting water are added to the oceans every second. As seas rise, wildlife and communities along the coast are increasingly stressed.

When icecaps and glaciers melt, the sun's rays aren't reflected away from the Earth, so global warming accelerates. This speeds up rising sea levels, flooding low-lying regions and coastal cities. This will most dramatically affect wildlife and poorer human communities. Whole islands and countries are now threatened by rising seas. Many climate refugees are already fleeing affected areas, leading to wider social disruption and conflict in places.

Radical cuts in our emissions of greenhouse gases are needed; and every little bit helps.

RIVERS

Climate change is having a dramatic effect on rivers in many parts of the world. As glaciers melt, water levels in some places can rise and cause flooding: this is happening near Lake Victoria in Kenya, for example.

In the longer term, rivers are drying out across all continents, with dramatic effects on the ability of people and animals to find or grow food and find fresh drinking water. In the Rwenzori National Park in Uganda, you can now go kilometers along rivers without seeing any indigenous birds or trees. In many parts of the world, women and girls travel miles each day to carry water for their households as wells dry up.

In Tibet, the glaciers are receding, and the snow line is moving rapidly up the highest mountains in the world. Together with dams which divert the remaining water away from traditional water courses, this is increasingly giving rise to droughts and famines across large parts of the Indian subcontinent.

MARSHLANDS & MARGINS

I love watching the great egrets who pace slowly through the marshes along the rivers near my city, catching fish and other prey. California has been in a state of drought for several years. The less water we have, the shallower our rivers and marshes become. This reduces the habitat for great egrets and kills some of the fish on which they depend.

This panel shows a healthy and strong great egret at the river's edge. But our overuse of water and fossil fuels is already harming fish and bird populations. A wide range of other species also depend on freshwater rivers, marshes, or ponds, including many which live in the water at certain times in their lifecycle.

Saltmarshes and coastal areas are also critical for many migratory birds and insects, as precious resting places on their long journeys. These need protection from industrial and other pollutants. Some companies, like LUSH cosmetics, are actively helping local communities to do this, carefully organising their business to support sustainable suppliers. We in turn can support such businesses, while trying to keep our consumption in check.

AIR

Everything that lives needs air. We breathe in oxygen and breathe out carbon dioxide. Green plants use carbon dioxide in photosynthesis and produce oxygen. This delicate balance has been upset by human activities, especially the burning of carbon-based fuels for industry, transport, or heating. Excess carbon dioxide adds to the greenhouse effect, which causes global warming.

Many species also move through the air: whether by flying, jumping, gliding, or drifting on air currents. Many of these are insects, and loss of insect species has far-reaching consequences for entire ecosystems. Threats to insect populations include habitat destruction, intensive agriculture, invasive species, pollution, and climate change. Insects provide a food source for birds, amphibians, bats, and reptiles, while plants (including food crops) often rely on insects for pollination.

Each creature has its own role to play in the evolving creation. This panel shows a beautiful death's-head hawkmoth embroidered in the centre. The background fabric represents water and air which are mainstays of life on earth, and the clocks represent time running out.

BIRDS

This panel pictures swifts flying wild and free above the countryside, towns, and cities, with their cries announcing their arrival. Swift populations declined over 50% between 1995 and 2016, partly because of a parallel decline in insect populations, which is their main source of food. They have also struggled to find appropriate nesting sites, as old buildings are demolished or renovated, and new ones are built without space for nests. Other bird populations are under threat from food scarcity or are poisoned indirectly by agricultural chemicals and insecticides.

Extreme weather events driven by climate change have added to the perils of long-distance migration. Swifts that breed in the UK migrate to spend their winter in Africa, south of the Sahara, where they follow the rains to take advantage of rapid changes in insect populations.

Motor transport (on land or air) also endangers bird life. This is because of both collisions and noise pollution: small birds rely on summoning help by their alarm calls when in danger.

As well as taking more general action to avoid harming the environment, some panel-makers are working with wildlife and ornithology trusts and have become tree wardens to protect bird homes.

MOTHS & BUTTERFLIES

Butterflies usually get more attention than moths because they are more likely to be around during the day and are typically more brightly coloured. But most moths are beautifully patterned, though well camouflaged. Some have feathery antennae and furry bodies.

Butterfly and moth caterpillars feed mainly on leaves, including grasses. They often eat very specific plants, which are not necessarily of the same species as the flowers from which the adults take nectar. So plant diversity is very important for their survival. Conversely, the job of adults (or imagos) as pollinators means that they are crucial for the survival of various plant species. They are also food for a vast number of other creatures.

The Dingy Skipper (Erynnis tages) is camouflaged on stony ground. As with many other insects, its habitats have largely been destroyed by roads and railways which cut through wildernesses and tore up vegetation that was their home and larder. Breaking up land into small patches adds to their vulnerability, as these patches aren't big enough to sustain much biodiversity.

Dingy Skipper

Erynnis tages

Status: Vulnerable

How can I help protect you?

BEES & OTHER INSECTS

Insects constitute up to 90% of all species of animals on the planet and more than half of all living things, but there has been a rapid decline in recent years. One study found that biomass of insects caught in their traps fell by 75% in the 26 years to 2014, and many species have disappeared.

Bees are particularly important pollinators, and different species pollinate different plants. Where bees and their environments are cared for, as in much of Slovenia, their honey and wax can be harvested. Bee-keeping provides income for humans and an incentive care for them. However, diversity of wild, native bee species is key for ecosystems and pollination; in some places, managed honeybees add to their threats.

Pesticides and herbicides such as DDT and neonicotinoids are major culprits with far-reaching consequences for entire ecosystems.

Like some panel-makers, we can campaign to ban these damaging chemicals where they are still used, in our own country and abroad. We can also encourage the presence of pollinating insects by growing flowering plants and patches of wildflowers (sometimes known as weeds), and by not mowing lawns as often.

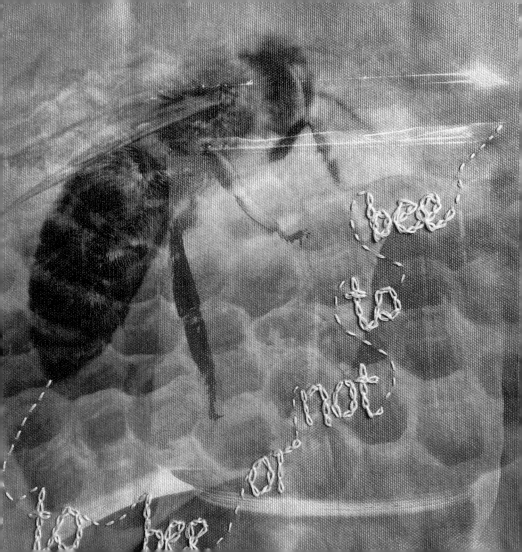

NIGHT SKY

Many animals sleep in the day and come out at night to feed, travel, and socialise, including several bird species, reptiles, mammals, arthropods, and insects. Darkness is essential for these creatures. But in the past century, the extent and intensity of artificial lighting at night has markedly increased, and light pollution has become a pressing conservation issue.

Migratory birds and hatchling sea turtles have been disoriented by tall lighted structures and other lights on their natal beaches, with catastrophic effects. Many nocturnal insects are attracted to light and may be trapped, burned or blinded by artificial lighting.

Artificial light can make many wild species vulnerable to predators, disrupting their food chains and preventing them from orienting themselves in time and space. It can also make it impossible for them to mate if, like the glow-worm, their potential mate needs to be able to see their bioluminescent flash; or if, like some frog species, they prefer to mate in the dark.

Reducing our use of artificial lighting will cut carbon emissions as well as helping nocturnal creatures.

When it's dark enough, you can see the stars.

HUMAN FLIGHT

Humans have been flying since the late eighteenth century, first in hot air balloons and gliders, and more recently in aeroplanes and spaceships.

Flying can be a rapid way to travel around the world, but unfortunately aircraft powered by fossil fuels release greenhouse gases, such as carbon dioxide, into the atmosphere, alongside soot and other pollutants. Aeroplanes operating at high altitudes can also release chemicals that interact with greenhouse gases, damaging the ozone layer and allowing more harmful ultraviolet radiation to reach the earth's surface.

This panel illustrates the tension between wanting to visit loved ones who live very far away and not wanting to add to the environmental damage caused by flying.

"We do not inherit the Earth from our ancestors; we borrow it from our children."
—Native American proverb

LAND ANIMALS

Ten thousand years ago, humans made up 1% of all land animals. The rest were wild. These days, about 32% of land animals are humans, 67% are livestock, and only 1% are wild.

Modern industrial farming practices – and the sheer number of animals involved – cause significant environmental damage, squeezing out wild species and accelerating climate change. This trend has increased dramatically in recent decades, as the number of humans has more than trebled since the 1950s.

This may be our downfall too. In many culture humans have styled ourselves lords or stewards over other animals, but we are also part of nature. We are vulnerable to food shortages and environmental breakdown, and we rely on other species. Instead of taking more for ourselves, we need to care for the whole planet; the balance of many living species, and future generations depend on us.

"There's a song that wants to sing itself through us. We just got to be available. Maybe the song that is to be sung through us is the most beautiful requiem for an irreplaceable planet or maybe it's a song of joyous rebirth as we create a new culture that doesn't destroy its world."

—Joanna Macy

TREES

This picture represents the interdependence of plant and animal communities. The jay in the foreground is planting an acorn for its winter larder, which may grow into a new tree. More than 500 plant and animal species depend on oak trees, not counting all the micro-organisms and fungi that live on oaks and enable the forest to thrive.

Women from different countries are planting a line of trees across central Africa. This Great Green Wall will help to stop the desert from spreading, securing animal habitats, retaining water, and fixing carbon dioxide.

Planting trees is essential, but they need to be cared for. It takes time for them to grow. So it is even more important to care for mature trees and not to cut them down.

"The best time to plant a tree was twenty years ago.
The next best time is now."
—Chinese proverb

HEDGEROWS & WILD PLACES

Wild and semi-wild places – such as hedgerows, forests, and riverbanks – can be very beautiful and productive. Myriad species call them home, with little or no interference from humans. We can marvel at their existence and enjoy the sight and scent of them, and many of their fruits, and we can be comforted by nature in times of stress.

Old forests, hedgerows, and wildflower meadows are also essential for maintaining genetic and species biodiversity and enabling adaptation in the face of environmental change.

However, 97% of Britain's wildflower meadows have been lost since the 1930s, according to researchers at Kew Gardens. Let us learn more about these places, protect them, and simplify our lives and habits of consumption so as not to add to commercial pressures on wild places.

"Consider the lilies of the field... not even Solomon in all his splendour was dressed like one of these."

—Matthew 6:28-29

TROPICAL RAINFORESTS

The tropical rainforests are vibrant and beautiful. They are home to many creatures and are essential as the earth's lungs. These 'carbon sinks' – absorbing carbon from the atmosphere – are tragically threatened by deforestation.

Deforestation in turn threatens to cause the extinction of many species including chimpanzees, gorillas, and orangutans. Indigenous people also suffer due to the destruction of their lands and threats to species on which they depend for food, shelter, and medicines.

Monocultures (whether palm oil, coffee, cocoa, maize, or grass) are counterproductive, as the land quickly loses its fertility. Lack of biodiversity affects pollination too. For example, the tiny insects that pollinate cocoa flowers simply cannot survive in a cocoa monoculture, so the flowers may need to be pollinated by hand if they are to produce cocoa beans.

WILDLIFE PARKS

At the beginning of the twentieth century, there were a few million African elephants in the wild. Today, that number has fallen to an estimated 450,000. Wildlife reserves have been established to try to protect elephants and other wild creatures, and international wildlife tourism is an important source of income in many countries.

However, this can cause problems for people living nearby, such as in the Kasese District in Uganda, where wild animals have disrupted agriculture in the villages adjoining these conservation areas. Payments are made from national parks to these farmers, but often it is not enough to compensate for wildlife damage to their crops.

Many tensions arise when we try to conserve wildlife while sustaining humans who are trying to find herbal medicine, firewood, and land for grazing animals within protected areas. The Peace Advocates Foundation in Kasese tries to prevent further harm by mediating some of the conflicts that arise. This peace-making work is a crucial aspect of conservation efforts in the region.

AUSTRALIAN CAMELS

In the 1860s, camels were imported into Australia by British settlers. Their purpose was to carry supplies for those constructing telegraph lines and railways. They carted food and other goods across vast expanses of Outback desert too harsh for horses.

Since then, wild camels have multiplied, and Australia has over one million camels. During recent droughts, wild camels sought water in towns and villages, damaging buildings and competing with humans and livestock for water. Because of this, many camels have been culled across Australia. Many others then perished in floods. This is a sad example of how the importing of non-native species can have unexpected consequences.

Australia's bushfires and floods have also become more violent in recent years, and already the country is facing an "insurance crisis" with 1 in 25 homes on track to be effectively uninsurable by 2030. These issues were critical in the 2022 Australian elections and are rapidly becoming more important elsewhere.

FACTORY FARMING

Farmed poultry today makes up 70% of all birds on the planet. This panel contrasts the rare happy situation of outdoor chickens on smallholdings with the reality of factory farming, which aims to create cheap food and large profits.

Most animals farmed for food have a nightmarish existence in unhealthy, overcrowded conditions devoid of natural stimulus; they are regularly pumped full of hormones and drugs. It is no wonder that those who eat them can develop antibiotic resistance, cancers, and other diseases.

In the UK, chicken mega-farms have also been polluting waterways with their sewage runoff, poisoning fish and plant life alike. Tighter environmental controls on farming, food, and environmental pollution are clearly needed. We also need to change our attitudes to food, to respect the lives and dignity of animals, and to avoid wasting food.

DANGER
do not handle

Antibiotics

FRAGILE ABUNDANCE

Many of us in wealthier countries take food for granted. We assume that it will always be available so long as we have the money. But almost all our food comes from living plants or animals, and these will not grow unless conditions are right.

I love to see the cornfields peppered with wildflowers and humming with insects and birdlife. However, industrial farming practices, with monocultures and pesticides, have made such scenes increasingly rare. Extreme weather events are also damaging yields and increasing food prices. Transporting food over long distances pollutes the environment and is increasingly expensive.

Many of us are now trying to buy locally-grown food and growing some of our own, avoiding chemicals and learning about complementary planting and more sustainable planting designs. We are also learning to plan and cook to avoid wasting money and food.

BENEATH OUR FEET

The earth beneath our feet is home to myriad life forms. Because it is generally harder to move through earth and rock than on the Earth's surface, some of these species evolve more slowly than creatures that live above ground, retaining great biodiversity.

Earthworms, roots, and fungi create clumps of soil within which smaller animals such as springtails and mites, and millions of bacteria and microscopic creatures, make their homes. The complex organisation of healthy soil enables water, oxygen, and nutrients to pass through. Trees, fungi, and other organisms communicate underground through the mycelial web, enabling forests to be self-sustaining for thousands of years. However, as the climate changes and pollutants and deforestation disrupt this community, many life forms are at risk.

Working the earth connects us with this community. We can care for it by avoiding chemical treatments and pollution, and by replacing nutrients taken out by agriculture through recycling (composting) animal and vegetable matter. Without healthy soil, neither we humans nor most of the plants and creatures we love will survive for long.

"Is the land a source of belongings, or a source of belonging?"

—Robin Wall Kimmerer

CITIES

More than three-quarters of the world's people now live in cities.
London is my home city, and I love it. But like many cities around
the world, its air is highly polluted, and it is threatened by rising sea
levels.

Built environments exaggerate the effects of extreme weather. Soil
covered in tarmac or concrete does not store rainwater gets very hot
in heat waves and the life forms in it die off. City life also uses a lot
of energy, hardly any food can be grown locally, and city wildlife is
increasingly rare.

Current economic and political arrangements in many cities are not
well suited to making sure their complex infrastructures are resilient
and adaptable in the face of climate change. Green spaces are under
pressure, and nature is being squeezed out. Yet these spaces are
essential for our physical and mental well-being, especially for the
less well-off who may have little or no private space.

Local governments, planners, and communities are key in developing
greener cities fit for the future.

SPREADING DISEASE

More than half of human infections will be exacerbated by climate change. Flooding can spread hepatitis. Rising temperatures extend the lives of mosquitoes carrying malaria. Droughts can bring infected rodents into communities as they search for food.

Many species, stressed by hostile environments, become more prone to disease. Three quarters of new human diseases are spread by animals, including many viruses. Global warming is making these more prevalent. Illegal trading of animals such as pangolins is one way in which diseases spread.

Animal movements need to be controlled more tightly so that outbreaks of diseases like avian flu in poultry hatcheries or among game birds do not devastate wild populations.

We need to learn about the local effects of climate change on disease, take early action to avoid health crises when drought or heat waves threaten, and work together across the world to protect the environment.

Pangolins are unique mammals covered in hard scales. They eat ants and termites. Sadly they are the most illegally traded animals in the world.

Illegal trade in animals encourages diseases to jump from animals to humans. These zoonotic diseases include Ebola SARS MERS and COVID19

POLLUTED TRADITION

The Ganges river in India is sacred in Hindu tradition and is thought to have the power to wash away sins. However, the women depicted in this panel are also exposing themselves to many poisons: you can hardly see the water for chemical foam, and it is full of antibiotic-resistant bacteria. The air is so thick with fumes that the far riverbanks are invisible. Air pollution contributes to the premature deaths of 2 million Indians every year. Half of this pollution is caused by industry, and 44% is due to vehicles and crop burning.

Air pollution harms people and animals all over the world, causing asthma and cancers, including many among young children. Poorer countries and communities are generally the hardest hit.

Many participants in the Loving Earth Project are changing their habits to travel less by car and purchase fewer industrial goods, but wider societal changes are also needed.

"Live simply, that others may simply live."
—Mahatma Gandhi

REWILDING

My children and all future generations have inspired my work towards
a rewilded future. We have taken too much from the earth and are
impoverishing the world our children will inherit.

Rewilding is one way to work for a sustainable future. It means
restoring ecosystems so they can sustain themselves. The goal is
to treat the land in a way that emphasizes its natural processes, and
to reintroduce the species essential to these processes, reversing
biodiversity loss.

Studies suggest that rewilding 20% of the land is necessary for this
regeneration. The WildEast pledge asks each of us to rewild 20% of
what we have, be it a window-box, farm, park, or city. Many Loving
Earth Project participants are doing their bit for wildlife in their
gardens or farms, and campaigning for wildlife-friendly environmental
policies. Let the weeds grow!

Heureusement pour nous tous,

des nouveaux modèles agricoles,
respectueux de l'environnement émergent
peu à peu et ont beaucoup à nous apprendre.

TREADING SOFTLY IN THE LANDSCAPE

If we are to bring healing to the damaged world, we need both spiritual and scientific understanding. We need a willingness to be open to change for the sake of ourselves and other creatures. Spiritual practices and communities, such as those inspired by deep ecology, can help us in this. These can sustain and inspire action. As the deep ecologist Arne Naess wrote: "The remedy... against sadness caused by the world's misery is to do something about it."

I will walk ever more softly through the landscape that I love so that it may flourish and so nourish all of us.

"The way to do is to be."

Lao Tzu

LOVING EARTH QUESTIONS

These questions are a starting point to help you focus. You can return to them as often as you wish, changing or broadening your thinking. You could focus on a particular animal species, a place, or something else. You may decide to find out more, and often it is helpful to work with other people. You are invited to draw, write, and scribble your responses opposite, or on a larger sheet of paper.

Think of something you love: a place, a creature, a person, a thing.

How will climate change and environmental breakdown affect them? Has it already?

What actions are needed to reduce the risk of harm?

What will you do to help?

In reflecting on these questions, you may also find it helpful to listen to one of the guided meditations on the project's website. If you would like to develop your response into your own textile panel, more guidance about this can be found on our website: **lovingearth-project.uk**

WHAT NEXT?

"Caring is the greatest thing, caring matters most."

—Friedrich von Hügel

In 1992, 1,700 scientists around the world issued a "Warning to humanity". They warned of damage that we are now seeing in many forms, and they said that much of the harm was irreversible. They explained that human activities "put at serious risk the future that we wish for human society and the plant and animal kingdoms, and may so alter the living world that it will be unable to sustain life in the manner that we know". They urged that fundamental changes in human ambitions and practices were desperately needed.

In 2017, after 25 years, this message was updated, pointing out that humanity had made almost no progress in reducing the harm inflicted on the planet by its growing population. This time, it was signed by 20,000 scientists. While some progress had been made regarding the ozone layer and acid rain, other problems had become far worse and new ones had joined them. Climate change was in danger of becoming a runaway process resulting in mass extinction, and soon it would be too late to change this.

The Intergovernmental Panel on Climate Change (IPCC), a United Nations body, continues to bring together science from across the globe. Specialist reports and summaries can be found at **ipcc.ch**. In the UK, the government's Climate Change Committee has published several reports advising on the measures that government should take to meet UN targets: see: **theccc.org.uk**

green energy
emissions
euse and
ecycle
single use
plastic
pesticides
Shop local
buy
organic
PATH WILL YOU
choose
litter

However, very radical changes are urgently needed if we are to prevent runaway climate change and ever faster extinctions. We need to stop seeing the Earth and its many plants, creatures, and minerals simply as resources for humans to take and use. To do this effectively, we will need new aims, skills, and ways of organising societies. We will need to collaborate with one another and with the rest of nature, rather than competing to destruction. Perhaps we need to be less busy?

Love can help us in this. But love alone is not enough. We need to understand the impact of our lifestyles and make changes. Understanding the creatures and places we love, and how these depend on other things around them, will help us take more effective action to prevent further harm and accept necessary adaptations. Some of the books listed on page 73 may be helpful in this. Yet we will also need to learn new skills: different ways of treating and drawing on and caring for materials, land, and one another. Trying to reduce your carbon footprint is a good place to start; **carbonindependent.org** has lots of useful information about this. Spiritual practices can be helpful too, both to challenge and to nurture us, especially if they focus on truth, love, hope, and remaining open to new insights and possibilities.

We all start from different places, with different gifts and opportunities. Each of us has a part to play in the bigger picture. Accepting that we don't have all the answers is itself a good starting point for moving forward.

> *"Humankind has not woven the web of life. We are but one thread within it.*
> *Whatever we do to the web, we do to ourselves.*
> *All things are bound together. All things connect."*
>
> —Chief Seattle, 1854

Each star we see in the night sky is in another 'Star System'. In our Solar System only one of the 8 planets can support Life as we know
That's right! Planet Earth is so special and we are the only ones who can save it.

Caring for The Whole World We Love

SCIENCE

SAVE OUR PLANET WITH

Palaeontology

Marine

THE LOVING EARTH PROJECT

The Loving Earth Project was started in 2019 by members of the Quaker Arts Network aiming to help people engage with the challenges of environmental change without being overwhelmed. Our deepest spiritual values, especially Love and Truth, and our creativity, can both help us with this, and people from many other traditions have since joined the project.

The project continues to be run under the auspices of the Quaker Arts Network but is open to everyone. It has been supported by many individuals and groups in Britain and beyond. Online resources and events during the COVID-19 pandemic helped to extend the project's reach and scope, and the project was listed among the "best cultural events in Scotland for COP26". At the time of writing, over 400 panels have been completed, and they have been exhibited in groups in a variety of venues, most of which are listed on our website. People continue to make their own panels, run workshops, and organise local events, encouraging and informing a range of actions to help care for the planet.

The panels are displayed anonymously, and anyone is welcome to join the project, whatever their textile skills or environmental knowledge. All are welcome to make their own panels adapting the resources on our website as necessary.

The Loving Earth Project is grateful for financial support from the Westhill Endowment, the Southall Trust, The Edith M Ellis Trust, as well as the Quaker Arts Network, several Quaker Meetings, and individuals.

Some further reading

Alexandre Antonelli (2022). *The Hidden Universe: Adventures in Biodiversity*. Witness Books.

David Attenborough (2021). *Living Planet: The Web of Life on Earth*. William Collins.

Cherice Bock (2022). "Faith Communities as Hubs for Climate Resilience", in *The Palgrave Encyclopedia of Urban and Regional Futures*, ed. Robert Brears. Palgrave Macmillan.

Christine Chan and Ashlyn Still (2018). "Sea Level Rise by the Numbers", *Reuters Graphics*, 20 September. Available at: **tmsnrt.rs/3qnCPCv**

Dave Goulson (2014). *A Buzz in the Meadow*. Vintage Books.

Dave Goulson (2021). *Silent Earth: Averting the Insect Apocalypse*. Jonathan Cape.

Robin Wall Kimmerer (2013). *Braiding Sweetgrass: Indigenous Wisdom, Scientific Knowledge, and the Teaching of Plants*. Milkweed Editions.

Joanna Macy, with Chris Johnstone (2011) *Active Hope: How to Face the Mess We're in Without Going Crazy*. New World Library.

Oliver Milman (2022). "Climate impacts have worsened vast range of human diseases", *The Guardian*, 8 August.

George Monbiot (2022). *Regenesis: Feeding the World without Devouring the Planet*. Allen Lane.

Arne Naess (2008). *The Ecology of Wisdom: Writings by Arne Naess*, ed. Alan Drengson and Bill Devall. Counterpoint.

The *Imagine newsletter* is a weekly synthesis of academic insights into climate solutions, available from **theconversation.com**

List of illustrations

The illustrations in this book are photos of textile panels 30×30cm in size, made in response to the Loving Earth questions. The makers' accompanying texts can be seen in the online gallery at **lovingearth-project.uk**

The headings used in this book don't necessarily correspond to the original titles of the panels. These are listed below, in page order.

ACKNOWLEDGEMENTS

This booklet was edited by members of the Loving Earth Project's Steering Group. Thanks also to Anna Gaw, Amanda Jones, Graham Gosling, Marleen Schepers, John Lampen, and Sue Tyldesley for their contributions.

Copyright of images is jointly held by the Loving Earth Project and panel-makers.

Published by the Quaker Arts Network.

lovingearth-project.uk

lovingearthproject@gmail.com

LovingEarthProject

@lovingearthpro1

quakerarts.net

Edith M Ellis Trust